Date: 9/6/22

**PALM BEACH COUNTY
LIBRARY SYSTEM**

**3650 Summit Boulevard
West Palm Beach, FL 33406**

D1803814

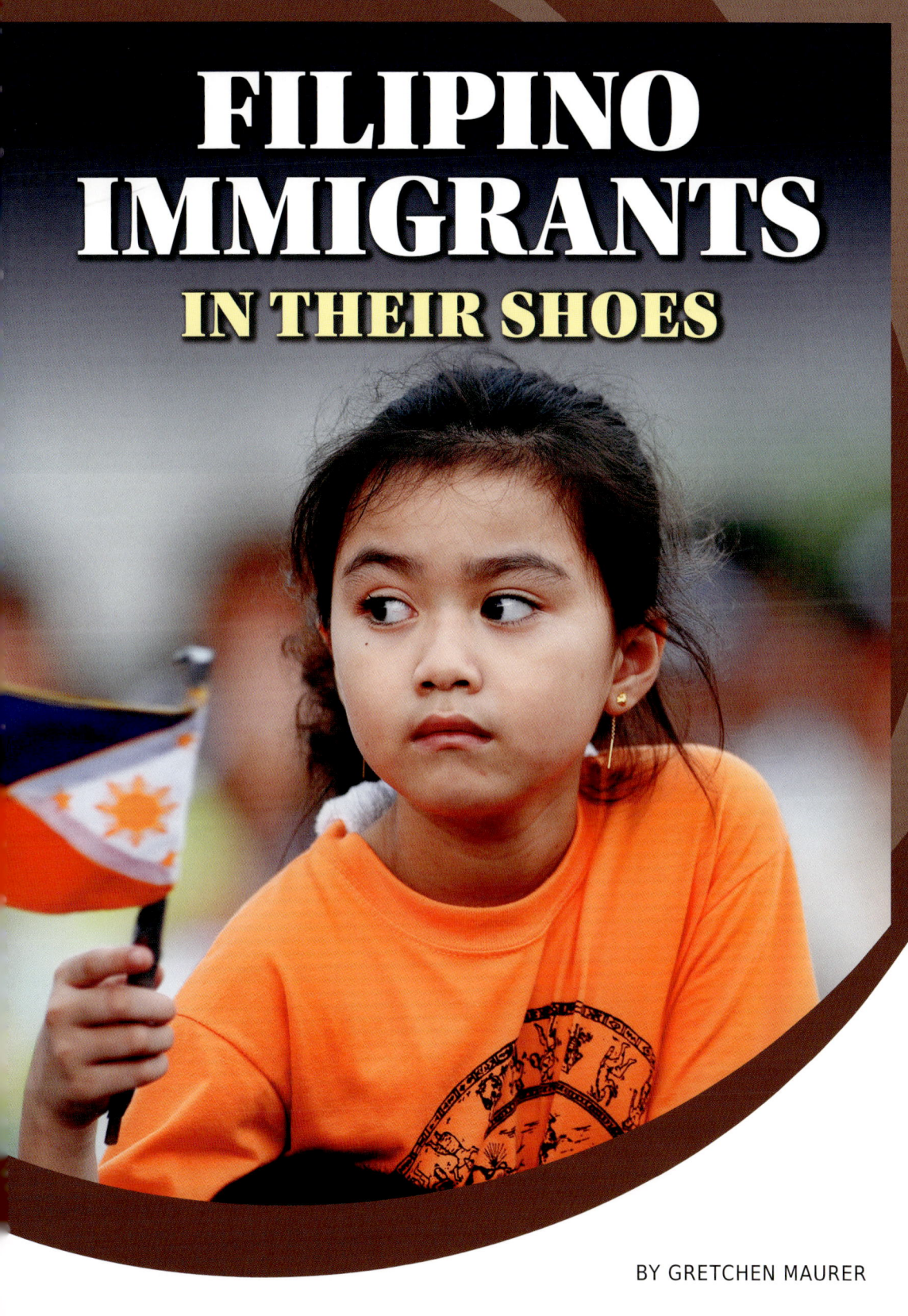

FILIPINO IMMIGRANTS
IN THEIR SHOES

BY GRETCHEN MAURER

Published by The Child's World®
1980 Lookout Drive • Mankato, MN 56003-1705
800-599-READ • www.childsworld.com

Content Consultant: Annalisa Enrile, PhD, Clinical Professor, University of Southern California

Photographs ©: Noel Celis/Stringer/AFP/Getty Images, cover, 1; Dorothea Lange NC History Images/Newscom, 6; Jon Bilous/Shutterstock Images, 8; Mark Elias/AP Images, 10; AP Images, 11; Manolito Tiuseco/Shutterstock Images, 12; Bullit Marquez/AP Images, 14, 22; Cire Notrevo/Shutterstock Images, 15; Paul Hawthorne/AP Images, 16; James Hagengruber/Billings Gazette/AP Images, 17; Jun Dumaguing/AP Images, 18; Rick Merron/AP Images, 20; iStockphoto, 21; Jacquelyn Martin/AP Images, 24; Red Line Editorial, 26; Charles Dharapak/AP Images, 28

Copyright © 2019 by The Child's World®
All rights reserved. No part of this book may be reproduced or utilized in any form or by any means without written permission from the publisher.

ISBN 9781503827974
LCCN 2018944219

Printed in the United States of America
PA02394

ABOUT THE AUTHOR

Gretchen Maurer is the author of several books. She lives in Northern California with her family.

TABLE OF CONTENTS

Fast Facts and Timeline 4

Chapter 1
Labor Leaders 6

Chapter 2
Professional Jobs 12

Chapter 3
Immigrants and the Navy 18

Chapter 4
**Growing Up in
the United States** 24

Think About It 29
Glossary 30
Source Notes 31
To Learn More 32
Index 32

FAST FACTS

Filipino Immigrants in the United States

- In 2010, Filipino immigrants were the fourth-largest immigrant group in the United States. Only Mexico, India, and China had more immigrants.
- Overall, Filipino immigrants in the United States are more likely to have stronger English skills, higher college education rates, and higher incomes than other immigrant groups.
- Between 2012 and 2016, Filipino immigrants in the United States lived mostly in California, Hawaii, Texas, New York, Illinois, and New Jersey.

Ties to the Philippines

- In 2016, 4.1 million people in the United States were either born in the Philippines or reported Filipino heritage.
- Most Filipinos move to the United States to reunite with family members or to seek better jobs.

TIMELINE

1903: Top Filipino students begin to arrive in the United States to study at universities.

1906: The first group of Filipino sugar and pineapple **plantation** recruits arrive in Hawaii. Workers endure backbreaking work, crowded living conditions, abusive bosses, and little pay.

1920s: Large numbers of Filipino immigrants begin migrating to the West Coast.

1934: Filipino immigration is limited to 50 immigrants per year, not including U.S. military or Hawaiian plantation workers.

1946: The Luce-Celler Act raises the annual number of Filipino immigrants allowed to move to the United States to 100.

1965: The Hart-Celler Act ends the system that had restricted Filipino immigration to the United States.

2005: The U.S. government seeks to bring Filipino nurses to the United States.

2016: More than 1.9 million Filipinos live in the United States.

Chapter 1

LABOR LEADERS

On a humid day in April 1926, 19-year-old Philip Vera Cruz stood on the deck of the *Empress of Asia*. He watched the pier in Manila, Philippines, fade into the distance. He had dreamed about going to the United States for years. He had heard great things about it from American teachers sent to work in the Philippines. Suddenly, though, he felt as if he were being torn in two. "I stood there until I couldn't see anymore where I came from," he said.[1]

◀ **Many Filipino immigrants found jobs in the United States as farmworkers.**

Like hundreds of thousands of young Filipino men during the early- and mid-1900s, Vera Cruz planned to earn a college degree in the United States. Then he would work, save money, and send it home to help his family. After this, he planned to return to the Philippines.

Nearly one month after leaving Manila, after surviving crowded conditions in the ship, Vera Cruz arrived in Seattle, Washington. He had little money, no job lined up, and no idea of what to do next. He found work in a box factory. He also worked as a busboy, beet harvester, cannery worker, and hotel worker. But he hardly made enough money to live on after sending money to his family. Vera Cruz studied and attended school whenever he could.

Adding to his struggles, Vera Cruz, like other Filipino immigrants, faced extreme racism in the 1930s. This was during the **Great Depression** when there weren't many jobs. Many white Americans believed they deserved the jobs and were angry at Filipinos. On July 29, 1930, a bomb was found in San Francisco, California. With the bomb was a note that said, "Death to all Filipinos!"[2] Carlos Bulosan moved to Seattle in 1930. He was 17. He saw the racism in the United States.

▲ Manila has been the capital of the Philippines since 1976.

He wrote, "I feel like a criminal running away from a crime I did not commit. And this crime is that I am a Filipino in America."[3]

In 1943, Vera Cruz moved to Delano, California. He harvested asparagus, lettuce, and grapes. He was unable to find higher-paying work. His dreams of earning a college education and returning to the Philippines evaporated into the 110°F (42°C) heat. Vera Cruz lived with other Filipino bachelors, or *manongs*, in small shacks in camps owned by the growers. The outdoor kitchens and toilets swarmed with flies and roaches.

When Vera Cruz bent over crops during his ten-hour shifts, his back hurt so badly he couldn't straighten it completely for days.

Vera Cruz read books about labor **unions** during his time off. Fired up by his knowledge, Vera Cruz joined a labor organization in early September 1965. The group was called the Agricultural Workers Organizing Committee. In September 1965, Vera Cruz and other Filipino workers refused to pick more grapes until growers improved wages and working conditions. The workers were officially on **strike**.

Cesar Chavez was a Mexican-American labor leader. He worked with another union. One week after the strike began, Chavez and his group joined the Filipinos in their cause. Together, they formed the United Farm Workers of America (UFW).

> "When [my father] comes home from the plantation, he stay[s] home for a few days or a week. He and his friends . . . would gather around especially in the evening. They tell stories and they laugh a lot. . . . When they finish telling stories, they play cards—Filipino card playing like 'Entre-quatro' or 'Hoong-kiyang.'"[4]
>
> *—Angeles Monrayo, a Filipino immigrant who immigrated to Hawaii as a baby in 1912*

▲ **Cesar Chavez (center) fought for farmworkers' rights.**

The Delano grape strike lasted until 1970. The strike won workers contracts from growers to improve work conditions and pay.

Vera Cruz worked with Chavez for 12 years. Vera Cruz was the second vice president and highest-ranking Filipino of the UFW. He enjoyed helping Filipino workers. However, in 1977, Vera Cruz left the union because of disagreements with Chavez and other leaders of the UFW.

▲ **Ferdinand Marcos ruled the Philippines between 1966 to 1986.**

Vera Cruz believed the union paid less attention to Filipinos than to Mexicans. He also didn't like that Chavez visited the Philippines in 1977 to accept an award from President Ferdinand Marcos, a harsh ruler. Vera Cruz felt this was a "slap in the face" to the farmworkers' struggle.[5]

Even though Vera Cruz never earned a college degree, he did earn the respect of farmworkers and leaders in the United States and around the world. In 1987, Vera Cruz received an award for his service to Filipinos in the United States.

Chapter 2

PROFESSIONAL JOBS

Luz Latus sat under a palm tree in the sweltering heat with her best friend. It was the mid-1950s. They were near her high school in Manila. Her friend turned to her and asked, "What are we going to do when we graduate?"[6]

Latus had already decided to go into nursing. She nodded toward the nursing school dormitory across the street. Nurses walked in and out of the building as they watched.

◀ **The Philippine General Hospital was built in the early 1900s.**

"Their caps, their uniforms. They always look so clean," she said.[7] Latus's aunt was her role model, and she was a nurse.

Latus's father wanted her to pick another profession. He wanted her to be a doctor, teacher, or lawyer. But Latus didn't change her mind. She studied hard in a university pre-nursing program and then trained at the Philippine General Hospital School of Nursing. Later, in 1959, she completed an undergraduate degree in public health. "Filipinos are **ambitious** people," she said. "We finish our education first before we think of the other stuff like dating."[8]

Around that time, starting in the 1960s, Filipino doctors, nurses, and other health care workers were recruited to work in U.S. hospitals, clinics, and nursing homes. The United States needed more medical professionals. Filipino nurses were well trained and educated in English.

Latus was always going to farewell parties for friends and family leaving for the United States, especially those in health care. She and others called it her country's **brain drain**. At the parties, Latus and her friends and family crowded around tables filled with food. Latus and her friends sang and danced to popular songs.

▲ Filipino nurses who graduate promise to take care of all their future patients.

Latus wanted to move to the United States to work, too. Still, she vowed to come back to Manila someday to help her community. In 1962, she accepted her first nursing job in Galveston, Texas. When Latus first drove through the streets of Galveston, she gasped. She had expected Galveston to look like the set of the John Wayne Western movies she watched growing up. But she quickly realized not all Texans were tall, and not all of them wore cowboy boots and hats.

Latus spoke English, but she found it hard at first to communicate with Texans because their accent was so different from hers.

In 1964, Latus married a man who worked in the U.S. Navy. They moved to San Diego, California, and she became a U.S. citizen. While raising their three children, Latus continued to work as a nurse. She also became friends with other navy families. Together, in 1979, they founded the Nayong Pilipino Association.

▲ **Galveston is located on an island off the coast of Texas.**

15

This was a social club for Filipinos in the United States. They organized a ball each year for the teenagers and went on picnics, where they enjoyed all kinds of food and treated the children to games and prizes.

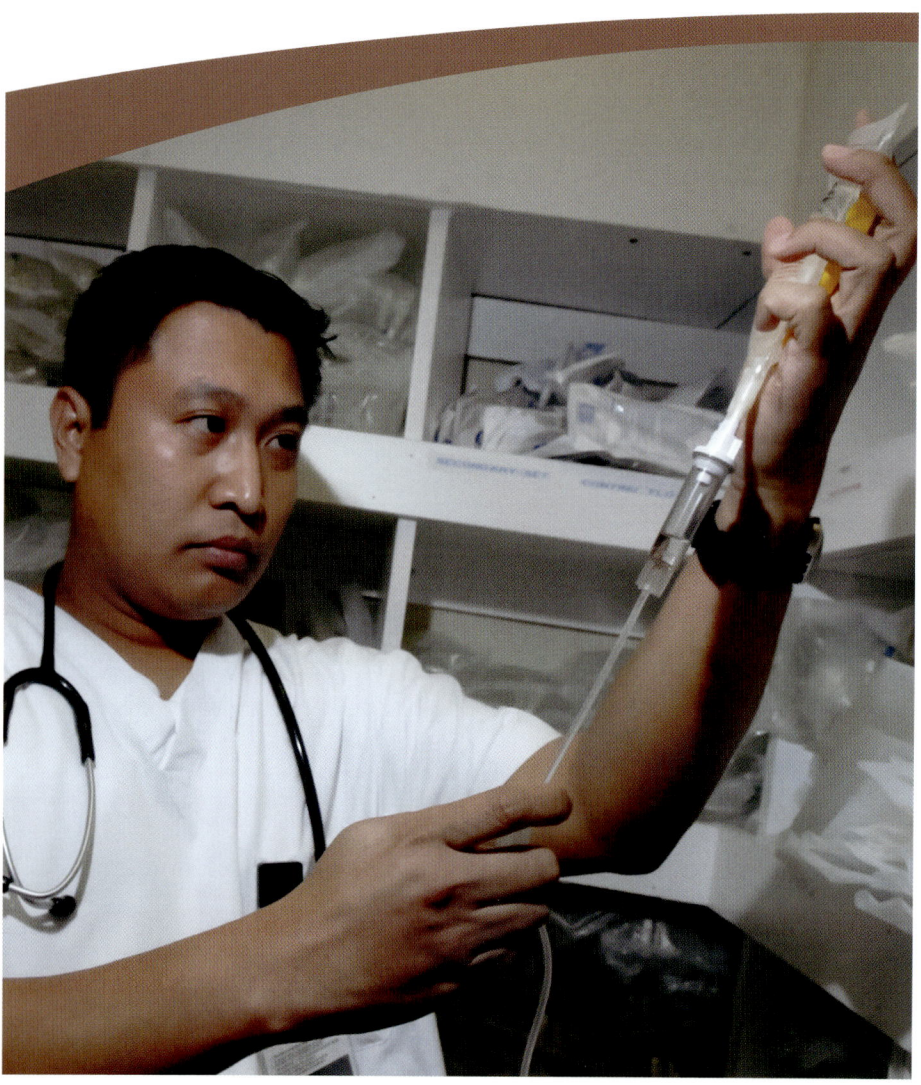

▲ In the 2000s, Filipino medical professionals continued to come to the United States for job opportunities.

▲ In 2003, Pamela Bioco (left) and Lilibeth Falaminiano (right) left the Philippines to accept nursing jobs in Montana.

Latus was awarded nurse of the year in San Diego in 1993. Unlike some nurses from the Philippines, she was never forced to work in a job she was overqualified for. Latus never made it back to live in the Philippines, but she said, "The Philippines is still home to me. I also consider the United States home, but if you ask me, it is more my children's country than it is mine."[9]

Chapter 3

IMMIGRANTS AND THE NAVY

Leo Sicat sat on a folding chair. He was in a large room on a U.S. Navy base in Manila. He was anxiously awaiting his fate along with 350 other young Filipino men. He was about to be interviewed by U.S. Navy personnel. Even though he had just finished studying chemical engineering for five years at a university in the Philippines, Sicat wanted to join the U.S. Navy.

◀ **U.S. Navy ships dock in Subic Bay in the Philippines.**

"It was the fad at that time," he said. "Most of my friends joined the U.S. Navy, they talked about the good life in the United States. To me, it was exciting."[10] Jiggling his foot to shake off his nerves, Sicat listened intently as officers called on people to start their interview.

Later that same day, Sicat was interviewed by navy personnel and completed the written exam. Soon after, he learned he was one of seven applicants who made the cut. He was so excited and proud.

Sicat joined the navy in October 1966. He welcomed the adventure and hoped to make a fair amount of money. He also looked forward to becoming a U.S. citizen. Filipinos in the U.S. Navy were excused from immigration **quotas** and could become citizens.

Sicat's excitement wore off once he learned that he and many other highly educated Filipinos were required to become **stewards**. After World War I (1914–1918), the navy allowed Filipinos, even those with a college education, to fill only low-ranking positions such as stewards. Sicat's steward training class was filled with Filipinos, African Americans, and "not a single white guy."[11]

▲ **People in the U.S. Navy served during the Vietnam War (1954–1975).**

In a large dining room at steward school, Sicat walked from table to table, placing silver spoons, knives, and forks in perfect, parallel positions as the instructor looked on. "We were taught how to cook and bake . . . set the table, and how to position the silverware, and the glass . . . the job of a waitress," he said. "Personally, I was so insulted."[12] The job placements weren't fair.

Some well-educated Filipino stewards even had to walk officers' dogs. Others acted as personal servants for officers' wives.

During the civil rights movement of the 1960s, people spoke out against about the racist policy. They knew it wasn't fair to limit people of color to low-ranking positions in the military.

▲ The Naval Medical Center San Diego has been around since 1922.

As a result, the navy created a new policy in the early 1970s. This policy allowed Filipino stewards to change jobs within the navy.

After this change, Sicat decided to attend hospital corps school for 16 weeks to become a navy nurse. He hoped he might make some small use of his science background. Later, while stationed at a naval hospital in San Diego, Sicat became a supervisor of admissions, overseeing the patients admitted to the hospital. Even though he wasn't directly using his science background, he appreciated the new skills he learned.

Over time, Sicat rose in navy rank. In 1990, after 24 years in the navy, marrying a Filipina, and raising three children, Sicat retired. He then sold real estate and insurance in Oceanside, California.

Although Sicat was originally disappointed with his first position in the navy, he was happy to be in the United States. "In my case, I sacrificed my five-year college education to become a steward in the U.S. Navy. But I have no regrets. Even if I had become a chemical engineer, there was no guarantee that I would have been able to get a stable job in the Philippines or to come to the United States," he said.[13]

◀ **Filipino American service members contribute to the U.S. military.**

Chapter 4

GROWING UP IN THE UNITED STATES

Sixteen-year-old Jose Antonio Vargas hopped on his bike and pedaled to the local Department of Motor Vehicles (DMV) office to apply for his driver's permit. Four years earlier, in 1993, he had flown to Mountain View, California, from the Philippines. He'd been living with his grandparents ever since. He loved his new home and adopted culture.

◀ **Jose Antonio Vargas fights for immigrant rights in the United States.**

His friends already had their licenses, and he was excited to get his, too.

Jose's excitement turned to shock and confusion as the lady at the DMV counter flipped over his **green card**, examined it, and whispered, "This is fake. Don't come back here again."[14] Jose jumped on his bike, raced home, and confronted his grandpa. Jose showed his grandpa the green card and asked if it was fake.

Jose's grandpa was proud man. He looked ashamed as he admitted to Jose that his green card was fake. He explained the situation to his grandson. He and his wife had moved to the United States in 1984. They were sponsored by his wife's sister, who had married a Filipino American serving in the U.S. military. This meant Jose's grandpa and his wife could become citizens. Ever since the Hart-Celler Act of 1965, many Filipino immigrants sponsored family members in this way.

Once Jose's grandpa became a citizen, he planned to get his grandson and daughter to come to the United States, too. However, he couldn't. Jose's mother was still legally married, even though she and her husband, Jose's father, were not together. Since Jose's mother was married, the law didn't allow Jose's grandpa to sponsor her come to the United States.

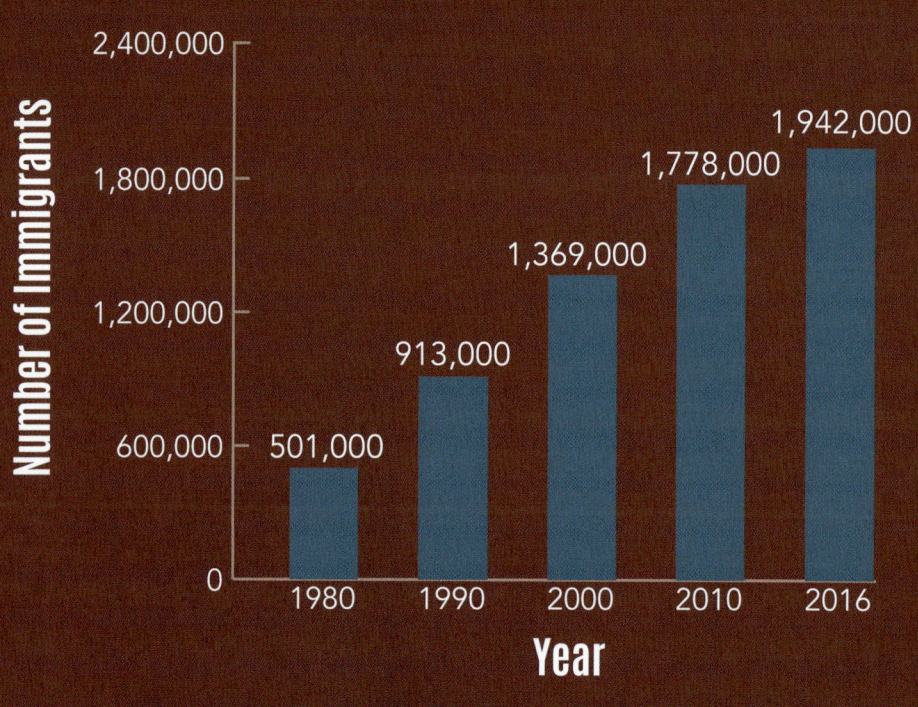

Still, Jose's grandpa hoped for a better life for his grandson. He discovered a way to get Jose into the United States with fake papers. He hoped his daughter would figure out a way to follow later. She never did.

Jose thrived in the United States, even though it took him a while to improve his English. One of his earliest memories in California was when a freckle-faced middle-school kid asked him, "What's up?" Jose answered, "The sky."[15] The kid and his friends laughed.

However, once Jose got used to American English, he did well. He never wanted to give anyone reason to doubt he was an American. He studied hard, joined the debate club, and won the eighth-grade spelling bee. He convinced himself that if he worked hard enough, he would be rewarded with U.S. citizenship.

Jose earned a college degree. He succeeded as a journalist for newspapers such as the *Washington Post*. He even contributed to several award-winning articles in 2008.

> "I tried so hard to blend in that I started to forget who I was. But the thing is, I don't want to do that. I want to be different; I want to acknowledge my difference. . . . I'm in the sky, in between America and the Philippines. Not belonging anywhere."[16]
>
> —*Jemimah Barba, an immigrant to Fresno, California, at age 12 in 2006*

27

However, he was never awarded U.S. citizenship. Since first sharing his experience as an **undocumented** immigrant in the *New York Times* in 2011, Jose has worked to help support immigrants. He has also given speeches at universities, directed documentaries, and written a book, *Dear America: Notes of an Undocumented Citizen*. "I grew up here," Jose said of the United States. "This is my home. Yet even though I think of myself as an American and consider America my country, my country doesn't think of me as one of its own."[17]

THINK ABOUT IT

- Do you think it's difficult for Filipino immigrants to adjust to life in the United States? Explain your answer.
- Why do you think so many Filipino immigrants settled on the West Coast of the United States?
- Why do you think some Filipino immigrants were treated badly after coming to the United States?

◄ **Jose has publicly admitted that he is an undocumented immigrant.**

GLOSSARY

ambitious (am-BISH-us): To be ambitious is to have a strong desire to be successful. Luz Latus believes Filipinos are ambitious.

brain drain (BRAYN DRAYN): A brain drain is one country's loss of educated professionals to another country. Some Filipinos feel their country suffered from a brain drain in the 1960s.

Great Depression (GRAYT di-PRESH-uhn): The Great Depression was a period of time in the United States between 1929 and 1939 when there were few jobs and people spent less. Millions of Americans struggled to find work during the Great Depression.

green card (GREEN KARD): A green card is an official card issued by the U.S. government to foreigners, permitting them to work and live in the United States. Jose Antonio Vargas did not have a real green card.

plantation (plan-TAY-shun): A plantation is a large farm on which crops are grown. Filipino plantation workers didn't receive good pay.

quotas (KWOH-tuhz): Quotas limit the number of people who are allowed to do something. Some Filipinos were exempt from quotas.

stewards (STOO-erds): Stewards are ship employees who wait on people. Navy stewards often work in the dining room.

strike (STRIKE): A strike is when people refuse to work as a form of organized protest. The Filipino workers went on strike.

undocumented (un-DOK-yoo-men-ted): Undocumented means without legal permission to live or work in the United States. Some immigrants in the United States are undocumented.

unions (YOON-yunz): Unions are organizations formed to protect workers' rights. Philip Vera Cruz researched labor unions.

SOURCE NOTES

1. Craig Scharlin. *Philip Vera Cruz*. Seattle, WA: University of Washington Press, 2000. Print. 56.

2. Dawn Bohulano Mabalon. *Little Manila Is in the Heart*. Durham, NC: Duke University Press, 2013. Print. 94.

3. Carlos Bulosan. *America Is in the Heart*. Seattle, WA: University of Washington Press, 2014. Print. vii.

4. Angeles Monrayo Raymundo. *Tomorrow's Memories*. Honolulu, HI: University of Hawai'i Press, 2003. Print. 82.

5. Craig Scharlin. *Philip Vera Cruz*. Seattle, WA: University of Washington Press, 2000. Print. 140.

6. Yen Le Espiritu. *Filipino American Lives*. Philadelphia, PA: Temple University Press, 1995. Print. 82.

7. Ibid. 82.

8. Ibid. 90.

9. Ibid. 91.

10. Ibid. 106.

11. Ibid. 108.

12. Ibid. 108.

13. Ibid. 107.

14. Jose Antonio Vargas. "My Life as an Undocumented Immigrant." *New York Times Magazine*. New York Times Company, 22 June 2011. Web. 20 July 2018.

15. Ibid.

16. Ram Reyes. "Between Two Worlds: The Filipino 1.5 Generation Immigrant Experience." *Rampage*. Rampage Online, 13 Dec. 2016. Web. 20 July 2018.

17. Jose Antonio Vargas. "My Life as an Undocumented Immigrant." *New York Times Magazine*. New York Times Company, 22 June 2011. Web. 20 July 2018.

TO LEARN MORE

Books

Brimner, Larry Dane. *Strike!: The Farm Workers' Fight for Their Rights.* Honesdale, PA: Calkins Creek Books, 2014.

Goldsworthy, Steve. *Philippines.* New York, NY: Weigl, 2014.

Mattern, Joanne. *Philippines.* New York, NY: Cavendish Square Publishing, 2018.

Web Sites

Visit our Web site for links about Filipino immigrants: childsworld.com/links

Note to Parents, Teachers, and Librarians: We routinely verify our Web links to make sure they are safe and active sites. So encourage your readers to check them out!

INDEX

Chavez, Cesar, 9, 10, 11

Department of Motor Vehicles (DMV), 24, 25

green card, 25

Hart-Celler Act, 5, 25

Latus, Luz, 12, 13, 14, 15, 17

Navy, U.S., 15, 18, 19, 23

Philippine General Hospital School of Nursing, 13

plantation, 5, 9

Sicat, Leo, 18, 19, 20, 23

stewards, 19, 20, 21, 23

strike, 9, 10

unions, 9, 10, 11

United Farm Workers of America (UFW), 9, 10, 11

Vargas, Jose Antonio, 24, 25, 26, 27, 29

Vera Cruz, Philip, 6, 7, 8, 9, 10, 11